How to Mash Monsters

Catherine Leblanc Roland Garrigue

INSIGHT KIDS

San Rafael, California

How to Mash Big Monsters

You may not think so,
but here's a news flash:
The largest of monsters
are the easiest to mash.

The biggest monsters
don't run very fast,
Shake them off easily
as you zip past!

Big heavy monsters are not smart at all.
Just point them in the wrong direction,
and without thinking, they will go.

Wide monsters can't squeeze through tight spaces.
Come up with a plan to block their way
and rest in your room, nice and safe.

Some monsters don't know how ghastly they look.
If one comes along, hold a mirror in its way
and give that big ugly monster a s p o o k !

Huge monsters are very impressive, it's true,
but with the help of a pointy pine needle
you can prick their massive foot,
and whoosh! They deflate and go KAPUT!

How to Mash Little Monsters

You need to be very observant to mash the littlest monsters.

They sneak about everywhere.

They crawl up the walls.

They fly onto your nose.

They slip and slide around your plate,

and cozy up beneath your sheets.

But you can't stop eating for fear of swallowing one . . .
or stop playing for fear of breathing one in . . .
or stop sleeping for fear of one creeping between your toes!

To get rid of little monsters, sprinkle sugar in a line leading up to a pot.
Wait very patiently at that spot.
One by one, the mini monsters will come . . .
and once they hop in, quickly clap on the lid.
Then you can make monster marmalade!

Tiny monsters may be strong in numbers,
but they are ridiculously weak.
In fact, they can't do anything to you!

Monst
Marm

sugar

They would love to have
just a bit of your muscle.
If you call them "scaredy-cats,"
just watch how they hustle!

How to Mash Medium-Size Monsters

Medium-size monsters are the worst, for they are well disguised.
They can look like anyone!
When you least suspect there's a monster around,
all of a sudden he won't leave you alone!

To get rid of them, ignore them at first,
something most medium-size monsters detest.
Pretend that they do not exist
and they'll get upset and finally quit.

If one still dares to annoy you,
take it by surprise and tear off its disguise.
Just grab a corner and the whole thing will come loose.
Revealed, the monster will immediately V a m o o s e !

How to Mash Weird Monsters

Whether they are big, teeny, or in between,
when dealing with the weirdest monsters of all,
here are a few tricks to keep up your sleeve.

Drooling monsters despise mustard.
With a smear on your cheek,
they'll recoil all flustered.

Prickly monsters are not crazy about glue.
If you spread some on the ground,
they'll get stuck and wriggle 'round.

Firecracker monsters
can't stand the smallest drop of water.
So fill a glass and sPlash!
They will crackle into a thousand colors
then fizzle out in a dash.

Grumbling monsters that want to eat and eat
are allergic to confetti.
Shower them with sparkles, and you will see
them cough so hard they'll lose their teeth!

Shapeless monsters are the hardest to fight.
They may seem impossible to beat,
but they do despise a blustery breeze.
So throw open the windows, and into the air,
the monsters will float away, along with your cares!

The End

To Louane, who is still a teeny tot,
but already strong enough to mash monsters.
—CL

For Thomas, Marie, Rémi, Hugo,
and Louis, my favorite "little monsters"!
—RG

INSIGHT
KIDS

PO Box 3088
San Rafael, California
www.insighteditions.com

Find us on Facebook: www.facebook.com/InsightEditions
Follow us on Twitter: @insighteditions

First published in the United States in 2013 by Insight Editions.
Originally published in France in 2008 by Éditions Glénat.
Comment Ratatiner les Monstres by
C. Leblanc and R. Garrigue © 2008 Glénat Editions
Translation © 2013 Insight Editions

Thanks to Christopher Goff and Marie Goff-Tuttle
for their help in translating this book.

Library of Congress Cataloging-in-Publication Data available.

ISBN: 978-1-60887-190-2

ROOTS of PEACE   REPLANTED PAPER

Insight Editions, in association with Roots of Peace, will plant two trees for each tree used in the
manufacturing of this book. Roots of Peace is an internationally renowned humanitarian organization
dedicated to eradicating land mines worldwide and converting war-torn lands into productive farms and
wildlife habitats. Roots of Peace will plant two million fruit and nut trees in Afghanistan and provide
farmers there with the skills and support necessary for sustainable land use.

Manufactured in China by Insight Editions

10 9 8 7 6 5 4 3 2 1